Where's the Silver?

Elizabeth could see the silver teapot, the cream pitcher, and the sugar bowl she and Jessica had played with, but she didn't see the sugar tongs. She tried to kick Jessica under the table.

"Elizabeth, please don't squirm," Mrs. Wakefield said. "Mrs. T. will think I haven't taught you good manners."

"I'm sorry," Elizabeth mumbled. But just to make sure that the tongs were indeed missing, Elizabeth edged to the side of her chair and stood halfway up.

"It isn't polite to leave the table in the middle of a meal, young lady," Mrs. Taylor said sharply.

With a desperate look at Jessica, Elizabeth sat back down. She had had a clear view of the tray, and the tongs were nowhere to be seen. Her appetite disappeared too.

Bantam Skylark Books in the
SWEET VALLEY KIDS series

SWEET VALLEY KIDS

THE MISSING TEA SET

Written by
Molly Mia Stewart

Created by
FRANCINE PASCAL

Illustrated by
Ying-Hwa Hu

A BANTAM SKYLARK BOOK ®
NEW YORK • TORONTO • LONDON • SYDNEY • AUCKLAND

RL 2, 005-008

THE MISSING TEA SET
A Bantam Skylark Book / August 1993

*Sweet Valley High® and Sweet Valley Kids are
trademarks of Francine Pascal*

Conceived by Francine Pascal

*Produced by Daniel Weiss Associates, Inc.
33 West 17th Street
New York, NY 10011*

Cover art by Susan Tang

*Skylark Books is a registered trademark of Bantam Books, a
division of Bantam Doubleday Dell Publishing Group, Inc.
Registered in U.S. Patent and Trademark Office and elsewhere.*

ISBN: 0-553-48015-4

Published simultaneously in the United States and Canada

*Bantam Books are published by Bantam Books, a division of Bantam
Doubleday Dell Publishing Group, Inc. Its trademark, consisting of the
words "Bantam Books" and the portrayal of a rooster, is Registered in
U.S. Patent and Trademark Office and in other countries. Marca
Registrada. Bantam Books, 1540 Broadway, New York, New York 10036.*

PRINTED IN THE UNITED STATES OF AMERICA

OPM   0 9 8 7 6 5 4 3 2 1

THE
MISSING
TEA SET

CHAPTER 1

The Mansion

"Will there be secret passages?" Elizabeth Wakefield asked, leaning forward from the backseat of the car.

"Or a ghost?" her twin sister, Jessica, added.

"Will there be paintings of people with eyes that follow you wherever you go?" Elizabeth continued.

"You'll see," Mrs. Wakefield answered with a laugh.

Elizabeth and Jessica shared a questioning look. Along with their mother, they had been invited to spend the weekend with an old friend of Mrs. Wakefield's, a woman named Mrs. Taylor. All they knew so far was that their mother and Aunt Laura used to visit Mrs. Taylor when *they* were little girls. And now it was Elizabeth's and Jessica's turn.

"Won't Mrs. Taylor be surprised to see how identical we are?" Elizabeth asked.

"I bet she won't know who's who," Jessica said.

It was hard for most people to tell the twins apart. Being identical twins meant they looked exactly alike. Both girls had blue-green eyes and long blond hair with bangs. When they wore matching outfits, even their best friends did double takes. One way to be sure who was who was by looking at their name bracelets.

The other way was by watching what they did. Elizabeth enjoyed playing soccer and softball, or making up adventures to play outdoors. She paid close attention in class, and always did her homework right away.

Jessica, on the other hand, hated to get her clothes dirty, so she liked playing on the swings or seesaws during recess. She was just as smart as Elizabeth, but she spent more time passing notes to her friends than she did listening to their teacher.

So even though they looked like two peas in a pod, there were many important differences between them. But that didn't keep Elizabeth and Jessica from being best friends.

"I wouldn't be surprised if Mrs. Taylor can tell you girls apart from the start," Mrs. Wakefield said. "She's very sharp. That always made *me* a little bit nervous."

"What do you mean, Mom?" Elizabeth asked.

Mrs. Wakefield turned the car off the highway.

3

"She's strict about manners. She's from the old school."

"Old school?" Jessica repeated. "What old school?"

Mrs. Wakefield laughed. "That means she has old-fashioned ideas about the proper way to behave. Her family was high society in the olden days. I remember her always telling us the proper way to hold a fork, or drink tea, or shake hands with someone."

"Do I hold my fork the right way?" Elizabeth asked.

"Don't worry about it," Mrs. Wakefield advised. "But try to mind your p's and q's."

Jessica made a face. "What does *that* mean?"

"It means look out, I think," Elizabeth whispered. She was beginning to wonder if their weekend would be *any* fun.

"You'll love the house," Mrs. Wakefield went on with a happy, faraway smile. "It's over a hundred and fifty years old, with wonderful rooms filled with exotic things. It always seemed magical when I was a little girl. I remember there was a special clock that played a lullaby at noon and midnight."

"Did you ever stay up until midnight to hear it?" Jessica asked, her eyes wide.

Mrs. Wakefield put one finger to her lips. "Shhh. Don't tell, but we did, once!"

Elizabeth didn't know if she was nervous or excited. They had been driving for three hours, and she knew they were almost there.

"This is it!" Mrs. Wakefield said.

They drove between a pair of tall iron gates connected to a vine-covered fence. The driveway seemed to go on and on, with towering trees and flower beds on both sides.

"This is like an adventure!" Elizabeth said eagerly.

They rounded a bend, and then they saw the house. It was three stories high, with turrets, balconies, porches, and several stained-glass windows. On one side was a fancy greenhouse. At both ends of the house tall evergreen trees grew like guards.

"It's a mansion," Elizabeth whispered. "Awesome! I can't wait to explore."

The front door opened, and a tall, gray-haired woman with a cane stepped out onto the porch just as the car came to a stop. Elizabeth looked out the window at Mrs. Taylor, and the smile slowly faded from her face.

Mrs. Taylor was the most serious, strict, and no-nonsense-looking person Elizabeth had ever seen.

CHAPTER 2

Exploring

Jessica shrank down in her seat and peered through the window. "Mrs. Taylor doesn't look very nice," she whispered.

"You're right," Elizabeth whispered back.

Mrs. Taylor looked down her nose, as though she stood on top of a pedestal. The hand that held her cane was covered with jeweled rings.

"Come on, girls," Mrs. Wakefield called cheerfully as she got out of the car. "Come meet Mrs. Taylor!"

She ran up the steps. Jessica and Elizabeth followed slowly behind her. As Jessica reached the first step, an elderly maid came out of the house.

"Gladys!" Mrs. Wakefield cried. "You're still here!"

"Of course I'm still here," Gladys replied haughtily.

"Gladys has been at my side through thick and thin," Mrs. Taylor said, speaking for the first time. She kissed Mrs. Wakefield on both cheeks. "Alice, how are you?"

"I'm fine, Mrs. T.," Mrs. Wakefield replied. She smiled. "I'd like to introduce my girls."

Jessica wondered if she should curtsey. Elizabeth just shook Mrs. Taylor's hand, so Jessica did the same.

"You must be Jessica," Mrs. Taylor said, her sharp eyes taking in every detail.

"Yes." Jessica was wide-eyed. "That's me."

"I'll get the suitcases," Gladys said. She

gave the girls such a stern look that Jessica's stomach flip-flopped.

"Come," Mrs. Taylor said. "I'll show you to your rooms. You might like to freshen up after your long car ride."

"Mom says we're already pretty fresh," Elizabeth joked.

Mrs. Taylor turned and arched her eyebrows. "Oh?"

Jessica and Elizabeth looked at each other and gulped. Without another word, the twins followed their mother and Mrs. Taylor into the house and up a wide mahogany staircase. Jessica sneaked a look behind her, only to see the sourpuss maid marching behind them with their suitcases.

"It's all just as I remember," Mrs. Wakefield said happily.

Jessica stopped on the second-floor landing in front of a table that held glass paperweights and a collection of beautiful porcelain pill boxes.

"Better not touch!" Elizabeth whispered nervously.

"That's good advice," Gladys said, catching up to the twins and breathing down on them. "Little fingers cause big trouble!"

Jessica nodded quickly and stuck her hands under her arms. "I wasn't touching."

Holding her breath, Jessica then tiptoed down the long hallway. She was worried. Mrs. Taylor was like an ogre out of a fairy tale, and Gladys was like her wicked servant. Jessica didn't know how she would last the weekend without being turned into a mouse or a lump of coal.

"This is where you girls will stay," Gladys said, pointing at an open door.

Jessica and Elizabeth went in. The bedroom had one large canopy bed, a flowered rug, and old country furniture.

"It's very nice," Jessica said, looking around.

"And cozy," Elizabeth added.

"Isn't it?" Mrs. Wakefield had come into the room with Mrs. Taylor. "Why don't you two explore the house now?" she suggested.

"Good idea," Mrs. Taylor agreed. "Your mother and I have a great deal of catching up to do, and we don't need children fidgeting around us." She held up her cane and pointed it at the girls. "Just be warned that my room is off-limits."

"Yes, ma'am," Elizabeth said in her most polite voice.

"And no running!" Gladys added.

Jessica backed up, bumped into the door, and then walked quickly out of the room. Elizabeth was fast on her sister's heels.

"Let's go to the third floor," Jessica said, dashing down the hallway.

Elizabeth raced up the stairs and grabbed the knob of the nearest door. "In here!" she said, pushing the door open. They both bolted inside.

13

"Wow!" Jessica stopped in her tracks and looked around. "What a gigantic bathroom."

To their amazement, the bathroom was as large as their bedroom at home. There were marble tiles, and gold-colored faucets, and even a bathtub with claw feet. The towels were stitched with a swirly capital "T."

"Look how shiny the floor is," Jessica said. "It's like an ice rink."

"Let's skate on it," Elizabeth suggested.

They sat down and took their sneakers off, and pretended to ice-skate on the marble floor. Jessica did a fancy turn in front of a long etched mirror. "This is fun!"

"Let's see what else there is," Elizabeth said.

After putting their sneakers back on, they tiptoed out of the bathroom. "I don't hear any voices," Elizabeth said.

"Good, the coast is clear," Jessica said with relief.

14

Every door they opened was a gateway to a new world. Each bedroom had a fancy canopy bed, and one had a cage of singing canaries by the window. Some had shelves full of books, and some had dust sheets draped over the furniture.

"It's kind of spooky," Jessica said. "But fun."

Elizabeth nodded. "And Mrs. Taylor lives here all alone, except for Gladys. I could never do that."

Jessica looked over her shoulder as they reached the very end of the hallway. "Let's go back to the second floor and try the rooms there. I'd really like to find that clock Mom told us about. I bet it's in Mrs. Taylor's room."

"That's off-limits," Elizabeth reminded her as they headed back to the stairs and down to the floor below.

"Oh, don't be such a worrywart," Jessica said. "No one will know we went in, if we're careful." She opened and closed door after door. The rooms were all lovely, but none was Mrs. Taylor's. There was only one door left. Jessica put her hand on the knob and turned it.

"I'm not going in," Elizabeth insisted. "It's too risky."

"Well, I am," Jessica said. She opened the door a crack and peeked in. The room was filled with portraits painted in dark colors. "Ancestors!" she said, sneaking in.

Elizabeth finally poked her head in and looked around. "Hey, maybe that's it," she whispered, pointing to a blue enamel clock resting on a vanity table.

Jessica tiptoed across the room and took the clock in her hands. Elizabeth came over to look. "You're right. This is it," Jessica said. On the back of the clock the word "Lullaby" was engraved.

"Too bad it's not noon yet," Elizabeth said. "I'd love to hear it play."

Jessica smiled. "We can. All we have to

do is move the two hands of the clock to the twelve."

With nimble fingers, Jessica did just that. Suddenly the clock began to play a lullaby. And just as suddenly, Jessica heard footsteps coming up the staircase.

"Someone's coming," she said hoarsely. She changed the clock back to the actual time, adding three minutes on. Then she put it down on the table, hoping whoever was coming had not heard the music. "Let's get out of here!"

As quick as mice, they slipped through the door and shut it softly. They were standing in the hallway, looking at a painting when Gladys turned the corner and saw them. She looked at them, then at Mrs. Taylor's bedroom door, and once again at the twins. Her eyes seemed to drill holes right through them.

"We're not doing anything!" Jessica squeaked.

CHAPTER 3

The Cave

Grabbing Jessica's hand, Elizabeth walked down the hallway as fast as she could without running. Gladys scowled at them as they went by, but she didn't say anything.

"That was close," Jessica said, going down the stairs.

"Don't do anything else that might get us into trouble," Elizabeth begged. "Mrs. Taylor looks so strict."

"Don't worry." Jessica was always proud of herself when she got away with something naughty. She opened a heavy wooden door and looked in. "This is the dining room."

Elizabeth followed. The room was like something from a storybook, filled with strange and unusual things. There was even a suit of armor standing guard in one of the dining-room corners.

"Look!" Jessica ran into the dim and shadowy room. "Isn't it beautiful?"

Elizabeth looked from side to side at the paintings, velvet curtains, and the enormous polished table. "I can't believe we're going to eat in here," she said, approaching Jessica, who was standing by a buffet, examining a delicate silver tea set.

"Isn't this the cutest thing you ever saw?" Jessica cooed, picking up the dainty silver cream pitcher.

"It is beautiful," Elizabeth agreed, noticing two other larger silver tea sets. "Everything in this house is beautiful. Come on, let's keep exploring."

Reluctantly Jessica put the cream pitcher back down on the silver tray with the teapot, sugar bowl, and sugar tongs. She followed Elizabeth. "Where are we going?"

"I don't know!" Elizabeth giggled. "We're on a jungle safari!" She led the way down a dark hallway, and then turned the corner. She gasped.

In front of them was a glass door leading to the greenhouse. Through the glass, Elizabeth caught a glimpse of tall, dark green leaves and feathery ferns.

"And there's the jungle!" she exclaimed.

She turned the handle on the door and swung it open. Together, she and Jessica stepped into the greenhouse. Tall rubber trees towered over them, and sunlight poured in from the glass roof above their heads.

"I see why Mom liked it here," Jessica said in a dreamy voice. "Mrs. Taylor is scary, but the house is great."

"Maybe Mrs. Taylor is nice once you get to know her," Elizabeth decided fairly.

"But I bet it takes a long time to get to know her," Jessica said. "Like forever."

They walked through the greenhouse, following the sound of trickling water. In the center of the greenhouse, they came upon a goldfish pool. Elizabeth put one finger in the water to see if the bright orange fish would come nibble.

"That tickles," she said, when one did. A shiver went up her back. "Come on, let's keep going."

Jessica nodded and pushed aside a tall fern. Not far away was another glass door that led outside.

"I want to explore the garden," Elizabeth said, leading the way.

Hand-in-hand, they walked out onto a manicured lawn. Rows of colorful flowers grew along neat cobblestone pathways.

Elizabeth could tell that Mrs. Taylor had a good gardener. Then she saw that beyond the delicate branches of a huge weeping willow stood an old, run-down stable.

"It'll be more fun where the weeds are growing," she said, heading toward the empty buidling.

Jessica skipped after her. "What did you find?" she called as she stopped next to a dense clump of bushes. Elizabeth was bending down, peering at something.

"I thought so," Elizabeth said excitedly. "It's like a cave underneath. Let's go in."

She crawled in under the bushes on her hands and knees. Overhead, the branches made a leafy roof.

"We can pretend we're camping," Elizabeth suggested. "Just like Dad and Steven are."

The twins' father and older brother were on a class camp-out while Elizabeth,

Jessica, and Mrs. Wakfield visited Mrs. Taylor.

"Wait a second," Jessica said. "We need some camping supplies. I'll be right back."

In a twinkling, Jessica vanished through the opening. Elizabeth crawled farther into the bushes, and discovered that there were several "caves," all connected by tunnels. She couldn't wait to show Jessica.

A few moments later she heard a rustling noise. She turned around to see Jessica wriggling into the cave backward. She seemed to be carrying something.

"What did you bring?" Elizabeth asked.

Jessica turned around with a triumphant smile. She was holding the delicate silver tea set.

CHAPTER 4

Tea for Two

"**A**re you *crazy*?" Elizabeth asked. "Did Gladys see you?"

"No," Jessica said confidently. "She was making lunch in the kitchen. I checked."

She put the tea pot, cream pitcher, and tongs on the ground, and arranged them in different ways while Elizabeth stared at her in shock.

"We're going to get into *huge* trouble," Elizabeth said at last. "Someone will see that it's missing."

"I bet they won't," Jessica said with a

smile. "There's tons of silver stuff in the dining room."

Elizabeth shook her head. "But we weren't supposed to touch anything. You should put it right back."

"I will put it back," Jessica said, pouting a little bit. "I'm not stealing it. I'm just borrowing it. Look, I even got some water from the goldfish pond." She picked up the teapot and poured murky water into the cream pitcher.

"Jessica . . ." Elizabeth shook her head slowly from side to side.

"Don't worry!" Jessica said, picking up the sugar tongs. "Would you like one lump or two?"

"I'll give you a lump on your head," Elizabeth said with a laugh. "OK, I guess we can play with it as long as we put it right back."

"We will," Jessica said happily. She was glad Elizabeth was in a good mood

again. Now they could play.

"There's a whole bunch of other caves," Elizabeth told her. "Do you want to see?"

"Sure." Jessica put the sugar tongs down and crawled after Elizabeth. "One cave could be your room, one could be my room, one could be the TV room and—"

"One room could be just for our stuffed animals," Elizabeth interrupted eagerly. "And another for real animals."

Jessica nodded. "We'd have our very own zoo."

"Eliiiiizabeth! Jeeeeesica! Lunchtime!"

Jessica stared guiltily at Elizabeth. "That's Mom calling."

"Quick, the silver!" Elizabeth said.

As fast as they could, they crawled back to the first cave. Jessica grabbed the teapot and cream pitcher and scrambled out onto the lawn.

"Hurry!" she said. Her heart was pounding in her ears. "We can't get caught!"

They raced back through the junglelike greenhouse and stopped at the dining-room door. By peeking around the edge of the door, Jessica could just see Gladys putting down a tray of sandwiches. Then she left the room.

"OK, the coast is clear," Jessica whispered. She ran in on tiptoes and put the silver back on its tray—just as Mrs. Taylor walked into the room.

CHAPTER 5

Polite Behavior

Elizabeth made herself smile when Mrs. Taylor looked at her. The elderly woman seemed to know every guilty secret in the world. Elizabeth's smile began to fade.

"I knew this would happen," Mrs. Taylor said in a disappointed tone. "I should have expected it."

Elizabeth and Jessica stared at each other. "But—but—" Elizabeth stammered. "How—?"

"Young ladies should wash their hands before they come to the table," Mrs. Taylor said, thumping her cane on the floor.

With a gasp of relief, Elizabeth and Jessica hurried out and found a washroom, where they both washed their dirty hands in nervous silence. Then they went back to the dining room.

"Next time we'll start without you," Gladys muttered irritably as she set a plate of salad in front of Elizabeth.

"I'm sorry," Elizabeth whispered. She didn't dare raise her eyes to look at Mrs. Taylor. She knew their secret would come out sooner or later. Probably sooner.

"What have you two girls been up to?" Mrs. Wakefield asked in a cheerful tone. "Exploring?"

"Yes," Elizabeth said quietly. She watched from the corner of her eye to see which fork Mrs. Taylor used. Elizabeth didn't want to do anything wrong from now on.

"We've got a secret hiding place," Jessica said mysteriously.

31

"There certainly are plenty of those," Mrs. Taylor said.

Elizabeth sent Jessica a worried glance, but her sister's happy-go-lucky expression didn't change. Jessica always got a big thrill from a close call.

"When I visited here," Mrs. Wakefield said, "Aunt Laura and I used to play hide-and-seek. Once it took Laura so long to find me that I fell asleep in my hiding place." She giggled.

Elizabeth gave her mother a faint smile. It almost seemed as though visiting Mrs. Taylor's house had turned Mrs. Wakefield into a kid again. Elizabeth wondered if her mother had ever done something as bad as borrowing a silver tea service, and decided that that was impossible.

While Jessica and the grown-ups talked, Elizabeth glanced over at the buffet. She could see the silver teapot, the cream pitcher, and the sugar bowl on the tray.

But she didn't see the tongs. She craned her neck for a better look, dropping the fork in her hand. It made a loud clatter on her plate.

"If you would like to speak, Elizabeth," Mrs. Taylor said sternly, "all you have to do is say so."

Elizabeth blushed. "Oh, um . . . Sorry."

Mrs. Taylor looked at her disapprovingly. Her face beet-red, Elizabeth looked down and toyed with her food. She tried to kick Jessica under the table, but her sister was out of reach. She stretched her leg and tried again.

"Elizabeth, please don't squirm," Mrs. Wakefield said with an apologetic smile for Mrs. Taylor. "Mrs. T. will think I haven't taught you good manners."

"I'm sorry," Elizabeth mumbled. She felt so guilty that even her ears felt hot. But just to make sure that the tongs were indeed missing, Elizabeth edged to the side

34

of her chair and stood halfway up.

"It isn't polite to leave the table in the middle of a meal, young lady," Mrs. Taylor said sharply.

With a desperate look at Jessica, Elizabeth sat back down. She had had a clear view of the tea tray, and the tongs were nowhere to be seen. Her appetite disappeared. Elizabeth sat in uneasy silence for the rest of lunch.

Finally, while Gladys was clearing the table, Mrs. Wakefield let out a contented sigh. "You know what I'd like? A nice cup of tea."

Elizabeth choked on her milk and began to cough. What if Mrs. Taylor used the tea service they'd been playing with? What if she noticed the missing tongs?

"Mom!" she gasped, trying to think. "Mom, it's a hot day. Too hot for tea. You should drink a glass of ice water, in the parlor."

"Now, that's a nice helpful girl," Mrs.

Taylor said. She gave Elizabeth her first look of approval.

Mrs. Wakefield smiled. "I think you're right, pumpkin. Thanks."

Elizabeth sat back in her chair with a sigh of relief. One more close call.

CHAPTER 6

To Tell or Not to Tell

Jessica stood up to follow Mrs. Taylor and Mrs. Wakefield out of the dining room. Elizabeth grabbed her by the elbow.

"Jess!" Elizabeth hissed, dragging her to the buffet.

"What?" Jessica stared at her sister in confusion.

Without a word, Elizabeth pointed at the silver tea tray. "What?" Jessica repeated, beginning to worry.

"The tongs," Elizabeth whispered, her eyes wide. "You didn't bring them."

"I know. I thought you brought them,"

Jessica replied with a tingle of fear creeping up on her.

"Well, I didn't," Elizabeth said. "Now we'll have to tell before someone finds out."

"NO!" Jessica grabbed Elizabeth's hands. "No, we can't tell!"

Jessica had a sudden vision of Mrs. Taylor growing to twice her normal height and laughing wickedly. "Mrs. Taylor would do something terrible to punish us," she wailed. "She might lock us in one of those rooms with the stuffed animal heads, or with the ghostly furniture, or . . ."

"I don't think so," Elizabeth said uncertainly. "But even if she did, it's still right for us to tell."

Jessica's mind raced in five different directions. "We can find the tongs!" she said. "We just have to go look for them. Mrs. Taylor will never know they were missing."

"But, Jessica . . ." Elizabeth argued.

"No. If we tell, Mom will be in trouble too," Jessica rushed on.

"OK," Elizabeth agreed doubtfully. "But we'd better start looking right—"

The door from the kitchen opened, and Gladys came in with a tray. She stopped and glared at them.

"What are you two doing here whispering and telling secrets? Up to no good, I'm sure," the crabby maid said.

Jessica held her hand behind her back and crossed her fingers. "We weren't doing anything. Honest."

"Well, go outside where you belong," Gladys snapped. Just as Jessica and Elizabeth were about to run out, she added, "And no running!"

"Yikes!" Jessica moaned, hurrying through the greenhouse. "Gladys is so mean!"

Jessica opened the door to the garden,

then heard voices from the nearby porch. She and Elizabeth froze. They could hear pacing footsteps, and the thump-thump of Mrs. Taylor's cane.

"Those girls must be quite a handful for you, Alice." Mrs. Taylor sounded very certain of herself.

"Oh, no," Mrs. Wakefield replied."They really are good girls. They're no trouble at all."

Jessica looked at Elizabeth. Elizabeth looked at Jessica. If they didn't find the silver sugar tongs, their mother would be humiliated.

"We'll find them," Jessica whispered. "We have to."

CHAPTER 7

No Table Manners

"Hurry," Elizabeth said, beckoning to Jessica with one hand. They raced through the tall weeds and crawled into the dense bushes.

"I'll look over here," Jessica said frantically.

"I'll look over there," Elizabeth added.

They spent twenty minutes searching all the caves. Elizabeth scraped dead leaves away from the ground, and checked under rocks, and looked through the soil until her hands were filthy and her knees were covered with dirt.

"Did you find them?" Jessica called fearfully.

Elizabeth was losing hope. "No. Did you?"

"No."

"Jessica?" Elizabeth crawled over to where her sister was. Jessica had muddy tears on her cheeks. "I think we should tell what we did."

"No," Jessica said, sniffling. "Not yet."

"But what if Mom wants tea again?" Elizabeth said, trying to be logical. "Or Mrs. Taylor? They might use *that* tea set. Then they'll see that the tongs are missing and we'll be in worse trouble. Let's admit what we did *before* we get caught."

"But . . ." Jessica chewed on a piece of her hair.

"If we're honest maybe we won't get punished," Elizabeth went on.

"Well . . ." Jessica's lower lip trembled as though she were about to cry. "Well . . .

OK. We'll tell. But not until after dinner. I don't want to get sent to bed without food."

For the rest of the afternoon, Elizabeth and Jessica continued exploring the house. But they weren't very enthusiastic about it. Nothing could bring back their spirit of adventure. By late afternoon, they were tired and sad.

"Well, you two look like you need some dinner," Mrs. Wakefield said, finding them sitting on the stairs. "Go on and change into your dresses. Mrs. Taylor always dresses up for dinner."

"Yes, Mom," Jessica said, not getting up.

Mrs. Wakefield gave them both a puzzled look. "What's wrong?"

Elizabeth sighed. "Nothing. Only . . ." She looked at Jessica, who shook her head. "Only . . . Gladys is pretty mean, isn't she?"

"Oh, is that it?" Mrs. Wakefield sat on the step between them and put her arms across

their shoulders. "When I was your age, Gladys used to scare me to death. She's such a grouch! But that's just how she is. Don't let it upset you. And as long as you remember your manners with Mrs. T., Gladys won't bite."

"OK, Mom," Elizabeth said.

She got up and climbed the stairs one at a time. Jessica trudged after her. In their bedroom, they watched the hands of a small clock creep closer and closer to dinnertime, while they put on their best dresses and brushed their hair.

"Ready?" Elizabeth asked.

"Ready," Jessica said.

When they entered the dining room, Mrs. Taylor was standing by her chair at the end of the table. She thumped her cane on the floor. "Again?" she asked in an outraged voice.

Elizabeth's heart jumped inside her. "Wh-what?"

"Those hands!" Mrs. Taylor declared. "You're as grubby as two boys!"

Speechless with nervousness, Elizabeth and Jessica left the room to wash their hands. In the washroom, one frightened tear rolled down Jessica's cheek. "I know Mrs. Taylor is going to punish us," she whispered. "I just know it."

"Don't be scared," Elizabeth said. "It'll be fine."

Jessica gave her sister a doubtful look, but followed her back to the dining room. Luckily, they were allowed to sit next to each other. Under the tablecloth, they held hands.

"You two are very silent this evening," Mrs. Taylor said. "Don't you have anything to say?"

"No, ma'am," Elizabeth said nervously. "I mean, yes, ma'am."

Jessica reached across the table for a basket of rolls, and knocked over the salt shaker.

"It is polite for young ladies to ask for things to be passed," Mrs. Taylor said.

"I'm sorry," Jessica whispered. "Would you please pass me some rolls, Mrs. Taylor?"

Meanwhile, Elizabeth looked at their mother, who gave her an encouraging smile. She smiled back, putting her elbows on the table. Too late, her mother shook her head.

"Elbows *off* the table," Gladys said from the doorway.

Elizabeth quickly did as she was told, but Gladys's sharp words made the fork in Jessica's hand shake. All the peas that were on it fell onto her plate and bounced off. There was an uncomfortable silence.

"Sorry," Jessica said again.

She leaned close to Elizabeth. "I can't do it!" she whispered. "I just can't tell."

Mrs. Taylor cleared her throat loudly, and gave them a stern look. "No secrets at the dinner table!" she thundered.

Elizabeth fought to swallow her mouthful of milk. It felt as though she had a rock in her throat. They were in big trouble already. It could only get worse.

CHAPTER 8

Tea Is for Grown-Ups

The twins still had not admitted their mistake by bedtime. Jessica put on her pajamas and got into the huge, lace-canopied bed.

"I know it's going to be awful when we tell," she said. "Maybe Mrs. Taylor won't let us leave. She could keep us in the dungeon forever. Mom, too."

"Don't say that," Elizabeth said with a shudder. She went to a table that held a collection of music boxes. "Do you want to play these?" she asked.

Jessica shook her head miserably. "No."

"Do you want to go out on the balcony?" Elizabeth asked. "Or make funny faces in the mirrors?"

Jessica shook her head again. "Don't try to cheer me up, Liz. I'll never be happy again."

"We should have told them at dinner," Elizabeth said. She got into bed too. "I feel dumb for chickening out."

"We'll look again in the morning," Jessica insisted. "That's all we can do." She pulled the blanket up to her chin. She was sad, tired, and worried. It was a terrible way to feel.

But she fell asleep anyway. . . .

Jessica was running down a long, dark hallway, opening the doors and glancing in. Each room was filled with strange things, like floating silverware, giant talking plants, and ice-skaters drinking tea from silver teacups. Jessica was looking for something, but she couldn't find it.

And someone was following her.

"Brush your hair!" a stern voice ordered. "Stand up straight!"

It was Mrs. Taylor. She was waving her cane in the air as she shouted commands to Jessica. "Don't talk with your mouth full! Mind your p's and q's! Don't fidget!"

Jessica ran on and on through the enormous house, but wherever she went, the voice of Mrs. Taylor followed her, and she never found what she was looking for.

"Rise and shine!" Mrs. Wakefield called out brightly.

Jessica opened her eyes and sat up in bed. Her mother was opening the curtains, and brilliant sunlight poured into the room.

"Good morning, girls. It's your last day to explore this wonderful house, so don't linger in bed too long." She gave them each a kiss and left the room.

Jessica felt awful. "I'm going to find those tongs if it's the last thing I do!" she whispered to Elizabeth as they went downstairs for breakfast. "Let's leave as soon as we finish eating and look for them again. Then I'll never touch another thing as long as I live. Honest."

When they reached the breakfast table in the kitchen, both girls said a timid good morning to Mrs. Taylor, who was reading the newspaper. Mrs. Wakefield smiled at them both.

"Would you girls like to have a cup of tea with your breakfast?" she asked.

Jessica stared. "Tea?"

"When Aunt Laura and I used to stay here, we would always have tea in the mornings with our breakfast," Mrs. Wakefield explained. "It made us feel grown up."

"But—why, Mom?" Elizabeth whispered.

Mrs. Wakefield shrugged. "Oh, I don't

know. I suppose it was using that adorable silver tea set that made us feel special."

Jessica couldn't help looking across the room at the door to the dining room. Her mother couldn't possibly mean *that* tea set, could she?

"I remember it so well," Mrs. Wakefield went on. "The cute little creamer, the sugar bowl and tongs, the tray, and the teapot. All so dainty and pretty."

"I'll tell you something, Alice," Mrs. Taylor broke in unexpectedly. "I never did drink tea, as you know. I always drink coffee, and always will. What I'd like to do is give you that little tea service as a gift."

Mrs. Wakefield turned pink with pleasure. "Oh, Mrs. T., that is so kind of you."

Jessica carefully put her orange juice down, and wished she could disappear into thin air.

CHAPTER 9

The Truth Comes Out

Mrs. Taylor smiled a very friendly smile. "Then that's settled. You must have that tea service."

Elizabeth and Jessica stared in horror at their mother.

"What's wrong now?" Mrs. Wakefield asked, seeing their terrified faces.

"What do you want with an old tea set, Mom?" Jessica asked in a high voice. "We already have a teapot at home."

"Two teapots," Elizabeth chimed in nervously.

"That's right," Jessica said, nodding

her head very fast. "One's even shaped like an apple. Why do you need another one for?"

"Because it's a lovely silver tea service, and Mrs. T. is being very kind and generous by giving it to me." Their mother smiled at Mrs. Taylor. "Thank you so much, Mrs. T. I'll always treasure it and think of my happy times here when I use it."

"You're very welcome," Mrs. Taylor said, looking pleased and happy. "I'll go get it."

A terrified silence filled the kitchen when Mrs. Taylor left. Gladys was loading dishes into the dishwasher, but Elizabeth was sure the maid knew something was wrong.

"Mom?" Elizabeth said in a hoarse voice. "We have to tell you something."

"Yes," Jessica said, tears coming down her face.

Mrs. Wakefield looked at them both in astonishment. "My goodness, what on earth is wrong *now*?"

At that moment, Mrs. Taylor came back in, leaning on her cane. Her happy smile had vanished. Instead she wore a fierce, angry frown. Nobody spoke for several moments.

"I lost it!" Jessica finally blurted out. Then she burst into frightened sobs, and threw her arms around Mrs. Wakefield. "I'm sorry!"

Mrs. Taylor looked at Elizabeth for an explanation. Elizabeth got goose bumps. This was the moment of truth.

"Umm . . . we—we were playing under some bushes in the garden yesterday," Elizabeth stammered. Jessica's sobs filled the room. She glanced at Mrs. Wakefield, who was beginning to look embarrassed and disappointed.

"Yes?" Mrs. Taylor barked.

"Well, we thought it would be fun to have a sort of tea party," Elizabeth went on. "And we sort of borrowed the tea set.

We meant to put it all right back, but we lost the tongs. We looked for them everywhere."

She stopped and gulped hard. Her mother was looking at her and waiting. "We know we shouldn't have done it, and we'll pay for the tongs out of our allowances, Mrs. Taylor," Elizabeth finished up bravely. "We're really, *really* sorry."

"Stop crying, Jessica," Mrs. Wakefield said in a brisk voice. "You should apologize too. Don't make your sister do it all by herself."

"I'm sorry," Jessica sniffled, her eyes red.

Mrs. Taylor looked from Elizabeth, to Jessica, to Mrs. Wakefield, and back to Elizabeth again.

"Come with me," she said, crooking one finger.

Elizabeth felt a jolt of alarm all through her body. It was time to take their punishment.

CHAPTER 10

Mrs. Taylor Gets Messy

Jessica hid her face against her mother. "No! Don't put me in the dungeon!"

"Jessica, don't be ridiculous," Mrs. Wakefield said. "Nobody is going to put you in a dungeon."

Mrs. Wakefield stood up and took Jessica's and Elizabeth's hands. "Mrs. T., on behalf of my daughters, I apologize. And they will pay for the tongs."

"Not so fast," Mrs. Taylor said. She marched out of the kitchen, her cane thumping beside her.

Jessica and Elizabeth shared a fearful

glance, but their mother pulled them along after Mrs. Taylor. Jessica saw Gladys fall into step behind them with a satisfied smile.

Mrs. Taylor led the way through the dining room, down the hall, through the greenhouse with the gurgling goldfish pool, and out the door into the garden. Jessica stared at Mrs. Taylor's cane as it went thump-thump-thump on the ground. Without a word, they filed across the lawn to the tangle of bushes near the rundown stables.

Mrs. Taylor stopped at the entrance to the cave and faced the twins. "In there?" she asked.

Jessica gasped. "How did you know?"

To everyone's amazement, Mrs. Taylor let out a chuckle. "I used to play in there myself when I was a little girl," she said with a mischievous gleam in her eyes.

"*You* were a little girl?" Elizabeth asked.

Mrs. Taylor laughed. "I certainly was!"

Then an even more amazing thing happened. Leaning on her cane, Mrs. Taylor bent down and began to crawl into the tunnel.

"Mrs. T.!" Gladys burst out. "What are you doing?"

"Something I haven't done in years," Mrs. Taylor's muffled voice came from within the leaves. "Who's going to join me?"

Jessica and Elizabeth looked at each other. Elizabeth shrugged. Then they both got down on their hands and knees and followed Mrs. Taylor. Their mother did the same. Only Gladys stayed outside, muttering grumpily.

"This is marvelous!" Mrs. Wakefield said in surprise, looking around at the green-roofed caves. "Why didn't Laura and I ever find this place?"

Mrs. Taylor dusted off her hands. The

mischievous gleam still sparkled in her eyes. Jessica could hardly believe it was the same person who had seemed so frightening before.

"Now, let's all look," Mrs. Taylor suggested. "Four pairs of eyes are better than two."

"But we already looked everywhere," Elizabeth said.

"Never give up, that's my motto," Mrs. Taylor declared. "Come on. Everybody search."

Jessica suddenly began to hope that they really would find the missing sugar tongs, even though she and Elizabeth had searched so many times. All four of them crawled around on their hands and knees, examining every inch of ground.

Suddenly Mrs. Taylor let out a shout. "Here they are!" she exclaimed. She reached out and plucked the silver tongs from a branch.

"How did they get up there?" Elizabeth asked.

Jessica felt her stomach do a dive bomb. "Umm . . . I just remembered. I hung them there so they wouldn't get lost," she admitted, turning pink with embarrassment.

"You did too good a job," their mother said with a laugh. She shook her head. "Mrs. T., even though you've got the tongs back, we all apologize so much. I can promise you the girls will be disciplined."

"Oh, don't be too hard on them," Mrs. Taylor said, giving Jessica and Elizabeth a kind smile. "I did something very similar when I was their age. I lost one of my mother's gold rings, and I thought I would get a terrible punishment."

"Did you?" Elizabeth asked.

"No. My mother was very understanding," Mrs. Taylor said. "She forgave me. So I forgive you."

Without thinking, Jessica crawled right over to Mrs. Taylor and gave her a hug. Elizabeth did too.

"You're not really mean, not underneath," Jessica said.

"I should hope not," Mrs. Taylor replied in her usual stern voice.

"And we promise never to play with your things without permission," Elizabeth said. "If you'll let us come back."

Mrs. Taylor looked at Mrs. Wakefield. "I think that can be arranged," she said, smiling. "Now, let's get out of this 'cave.' I'm a little too old to be crawling around on my hands and knees all morning."

Filled with happiness and relief, Jessica led the way out. Gladys was standing at the entrance to the cave, frowning in disapproval.

"I knew you kids would get into mischief," the maid said.

Mrs. Taylor poked her head out of the

branches. "Oh, don't be such an old grouch, Gladys. And don't just stand there. Give me a hand!"

Jessica and Elizabeth both rushed forward to help Mrs. Taylor stand up.

"Now go on and play," the elderly woman said. "And remember, no more tea parties. Scoot!"

Laughing, Jessica and Elizabeth ran back into the wonderful, fairy-tale house. Now they could *really* explore!

After rambling over the whole house again from top to bottom, Elizabeth led the way to the library. "I bet there are some really interesting books in here," she said.

Jessica looked at the shelves full of thick, dusty books and made a face. "Who wants to look at books?"

"Some are really neat." Elizabeth stood on a chair to get *The Almanac of Ghouls and Goblins* from the shelf where she had seen it.

"Steven will be jealous that he didn't get to see this," Elizabeth said, flipping eagerly through the pages.

Jessica looked over Elizabeth's shoulder as her sister stepped down. Each page had a color illustration of some horrendous monster from mythologies or legends. Some of them were so terrifying that a shiver went up her spine.

"Let's look at something else," Jessica said nervously.

"Why?" Elizabeth smiled. "You're not scared, are you?"

Jessica shook her head slowly. "No," she fibbed, crossing her fingers behind her back. She closed her eyes for a moment, but all she saw was an image of a frightening monster. Her eyes flew open again.

"What's wrong?" Elizabeth asked.

"Nothing," Jessica said, looking over her

shoulder with another shiver. "Nothing at all."

Will all the pictures of monsters give Jessica bad dreams? Find out in Sweet Valley Kids #42, JESSICA'S MONSTER NIGHTMARE.

SWEET VALLEY KIDS

Jessica and Elizabeth have had lots of adventures in *Sweet Valley High* and *Sweet Valley Twins*...now read about the twins at age seven! You'll love all the fun that comes with being seven—birthday parties, playing dress-up, class projects, putting on puppet shows and plays, losing a tooth, setting up lemonade stands, caring for animals and much more! It's all part of SWEET VALLEY KIDS. Read them all!

☐	JESSICA AND THE SPELLING-BEE SURPRISE #21	15917-8	$2.75
☐	SWEET VALLEY SLUMBER PARTY #22	15934-8	$2.99
☐	LILA'S HAUNTED HOUSE PARTY # 23	15919-4	$2.99
☐	COUSIN KELLY'S FAMILY SECRET # 24	15920-8	$2.99
☐	LEFT-OUT ELIZABETH # 25	15921-6	$2.99
☐	JESSICA'S SNOBBY CLUB # 26	15922-4	$2.99
☐	THE SWEET VALLEY CLEANUP TEAM # 27	15923-2	$2.99
☐	ELIZABETH MEETS HER HERO #28	15924-0	$2.99
☐	ANDY AND THE ALIEN # 29	15925-9	$2.99
☐	JESSICA'S UNBURIED TREASURE # 30	15926-7	$2.99
☐	ELIZABETH AND JESSICA RUN AWAY # 31	48004-9	$2.99
☐	LEFT BACK! #32	48005-7	$2.99
☐	CAROLINE'S HALLOWEEN SPELL # 33	48006-5	$2.99
☐	THE BEST THANKSGIVING EVER # 34	48007-3	$2.99
☐	ELIZABETH'S BROKEN ARM # 35	48009-X	$2.99
☐	ELIZABETH'S VIDEO FEVER # 36	48010-3	$2.99
☐	THE BIG RACE # 37	48011-1	$2.99
☐	GOODBYE, EVA? # 38	48012-X	$2.99
☐	ELLEN IS HOME ALONE # 39	48013-8	$2.99